Friendship Rocks

FRIENDS SUPPORT Each Other

by **Megan Borgert-Spaniol**

PEBBLE
a capstone imprint

Published by Pebble, an imprint of Capstone.
1710 Roe Crest Drive
North Mankato, Minnesota 56003
capstonepub.com

Library of Congress Cataloging-in-Publication Data
Names: Borgert-Spaniol, Megan, 1989- author.
Title: Friends support each other / Megan Borgert-Spaniol.
Description: North Mankato : Pebble, 2022. | Series: Friendship rocks | Includes bibliographical references and index. | Audience: Ages 5-8 | Audience: Grades K-1 | Summary: "We all have problems that need solving. We also have triumphs that need celebrating! A good friend sticks with us through good and bad. They cheer us up when we're down and cheer us on when we're doing well. Learn how to be a good friend by supporting others!"— Provided by publisher.
Identifiers: LCCN 2021029841 (print) | LCCN 2021029842 (ebook) | ISBN 9781666315585 (hardcover) | ISBN 9781666320121 (paperback) | ISBN 9781666315646 (pdf) | ISBN 9781666315769 (kindle edition)
Subjects: LCSH: Friendship—Juvenile literature. | Helping behavior—Juvenile literature. | Interpersonal relations—Juvenile literature.
Classification: LCC BF575.F66 B667 2022 (print) | LCC BF575.F66 (ebook) | DDC 158.2/5—dc23
LC record available at https://lccn.loc.gov/2021029841
LC ebook record available at https://lccn.loc.gov/2021029842

Editorial and Design Credits
Editor: Jessica Rusick, Mighty Media; Designer: Aruna Rangarajan, Mighty Media

Image Credits
Shutterstock: CREATISTA, 15, Jacek Chabraszewski, 21, Lopolo, 19, matimix, 13, Monkey Business Images, 6, 7, Patrick Foto, Photographee.eu, 11, Pond Saksit, Cover, SeventyFour, 5, Sudowoodo, 20, wavebreakmedia, 9, 17

Design Elements: Mighty Media, Inc.

All internet sites appearing in back matter were available and accurate when this book was sent to press.

Printed in the United States 6732

TABLE OF CONTENTS

Words in **bold** are in the glossary.

The Lead Role

Your friend tries out for the school play. She wants the lead role. But she gets a small part. Your friend is sad.

You support your friend. You point out that her role has funny lines. Supporting a friend means cheering them up. It also means helping and rooting for them.

Helpful Support

Support makes us feel cared for. Support can also help us **succeed**! You and your friend are on a baseball team. She is **nervous** before the first game.

You play catch to help her practice. You tell her she will do great. This helps her feel better!

Help Without Being Asked

Sometimes we don't know how to ask for support. You are doing an **obstacle course** in gym. You notice your friend is moving slowly. He looks like he is hurt.

Don't wait for him to ask for help. Ask if he is okay. Then help him tell a teacher that he is hurt.

Quiet Support

Your friend might have a problem you can't fix. Maybe she is sad because her pet died. You may not know what to say. But you can still support her.

Sit with your friend. Listen to her. Ask if she wants a hug. Does she want to be alone? Then let her be by herself.

Cheer Them On

People need support when they feel sad. They also need support when they do well. Your friend scored the winning goal at a soccer game. You are happy for him. You give him a high five!

You Before Me

Supporting your friends isn't always easy. You **invite** your friend to a sleepover. At bedtime, she starts feeling homesick.

Your friend decides to go home. You feel sad. But you tell her you understand. You can try a sleepover another time.

Mistakes Happen

Support your friends even when they make **mistakes**. Your friend is acting goofy in the library. She drops her books.

Your friend is **embarrassed**. You don't make fun of her. You help instead! You pick up your friend's books.

Stand Up

Supporting friends also means standing up for them. Your friend wore new glasses to school. Your classmates **tease** him. You can tell your friend's feelings are hurt.

You stand up for your friend. You tell the others to stop teasing. Then you say you like his glasses!

Practice Being Supportive

We need support whether we do well or mess up. Practice giving support by cheering on a friend!

1. Stand across from your friend in an open space.
2. Gently toss a ball back and forth.
3. Every time one person catches the ball, the other person cheers in support.

4. Every time one person misses the ball, the other person says a positive message in support. This could be, "It's OK!" or "Keep working hard!"

5. Continue tossing the ball and cheering each other on for at least two minutes.

Glossary

embarrassed (em-BAR-uhst)—feeling silly or foolish in front of others

invite (in-VITE)—to ask someone to do something or go somewhere

mistake (muh-STAKE)—something done incorrectly

nervous (NUR-vuhss)—being afraid or worried about what will happen

obstacle course (OB-stuh-kuhl KORSS)—a series of objects that people must go over, under, or through

succeed (suhk-SEED)—to do well

tease (TEEZ)—to make fun of someone

Read More

Borgert-Spaniol, Megan. *Friends Accept You.* North Mankato, MN: Capstone, 2022.

Lee, Britney Winn. *The Boy with Big, Big Feelings*. Minneapolis: Beaming Books, 2019.

Miller, Pat Zietlow. *Be Kind*. New York: Roaring Brook Press, 2018.

Internet Sites

KidsHealth: Dealing with Bullies
kidshealth.org/en/kids/bullies.html?WT.ac=ctg#catemotion

PBSKids: Clifford the Big Red Dog—All around Birdwell
pbskids.org/clifford/games/all-around-birdwell

PBSKids Talk About: Kindness
pbskids.org/video/dots-spot/3017811961

Index

About the Author

Megan Borgert-Spaniol is an author and editor of children's media. When she isn't writing or reading, she enjoys doing yoga, eating croissants, and crafting homemade pizzas. Megan lives in Minneapolis, Minnesota, with a tall, goofy man and a small, chatty cat.